KU-795-652

For Frank, who fed the foxes

This paperback edition first published in 2007 by Andersen Press Ltd.
First published in Great Britain in 2006 by Andersen Press Ltd, 20 Vauxhall Bridge Road, London SW1V 2SA.
Published in Australia by Random House Australia Pty., Level 3, 100 Pacific Highway, North Sydney, NSW 2060.
Copyright © Michael Foreman, 2006 .
The rights of Michael Foreman to be identified as the author and illustrator of this work
have been asserted by him in accordance with the Copyright, Designs and Patents Act, 1988.
All rights reserved. Colour separated in Switzerland by Photolitho AG, Zürich.
Printed and bound in Italy by Grafiche AZ, Verona.

10   9   8   7   6   5   4   3   2

British Library Cataloguing in Publication Data available.

ISBN 978 1 84270 610 7

This book has been printed on acid-free paper

3 8015 02133 6536

Croydon Children's Libraries

P

You are welcome to borrow this book for up to 28 days.
Please return or renew it by the latest date stamped below.
You may renew books in person, by phoning 0208 726 6900
or via the Council's website www.croydon.gov.uk

Purley Children's Library
020 8660 1171

		3 0 DEC 2014
1 APR 2008	2 0 MAR 2010	
1 6 JUN 2008	2 6 MAR 2010	-9 AUG 2014
0 1 SEP 2008	2 4 AUG 2010	
2 SEP 2008	7 MAR 2011	
3 FEB 2008	7 JAN 2012	
	1 5 MAY 2012	
1 6 MAR 2009		
	1 7 NOV 2012	
1 2 OCT 2009	3 1 JAN 2013	
2 9 DEC 2009	-1 NOV 2013	

CROYDON
COUNCIL
www.croydon.gov.uk

Fox Tale

MICHAEL FOREMAN

Andersen Press • London

Mother always kept us warm
and safe. Father went hunting
in the night and brought us food
at dawn.

I will never forget the first time
I peeped outside our den. The air
was so fresh it took my breath away.

The birds were singing to the
rising sun and a cool breeze rustled
the leaves of early spring.

The breeze suddenly became a roaring, rattling whirlwind which raced towards me.

I tumbled back into the safety of our den under the ground and snuggled up to Mother and my brother and sister.

I had heard the whirlwind roaring before but always felt safe in our home.

Later in the day, Mother took us all outside and we lay together in the cover of the bushes and watched the brightly coloured whirlwinds race by.

When spring turned into summer, Mother took us out at night. The whirlwinds were still and the moonlit world was quiet.

She showed us where to find good things to eat. Some food we could just pick up and some we had to climb for. And some we had to catch! She told us never, ever, to go on the tracks of the whirlwinds.

Then, on an evening of mist and falling leaves, we went out with Father. The whirlwinds were still rattling and roaring but we felt safe with him.

We went to the place where the whirlwinds stop. It was very busy.

We watched and waited, and then Father's ears pricked up. A man came towards us. I wondered how he knew where we were.

He smiled when he saw
Father, and his smile grew
even wider when he saw us.
He took food from his bag;
some of our favourite things.
It was food Father had often
brought home to us. Now I
knew where it had come from.

Every evening after that,
Father took us to meet the
man, and each time he had
something tasty for us.

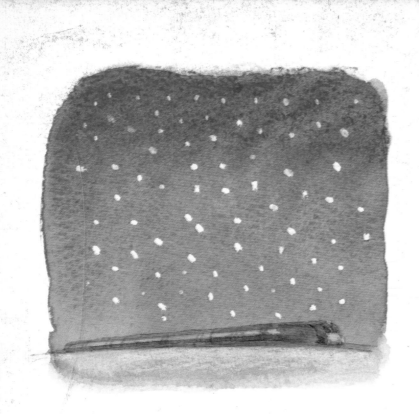

One evening when the man came down from the whirlwind, the world was white. We waited for him as usual but man-cubs began throwing white stuff at us.

The man ran to stop them, but slipped and fell. The man-cubs laughed and crowded around him, snatched his bag and looked inside. Then they threw it on the ground.

Father raced forwards and we followed. I thought Father was going for the food, but he snarled and showed his teeth, so we did the same and chased the man-cubs off into the darkness.

The man was still lying on the icy ground and I licked his hand. Father licked his face.

Then, another whirlwind arrived and people came. From the dark we watched as the man was carried away to a bright flashing light.

We waited for the man the next evening. He didn't come, but I saw one of the man-cubs standing in the shadows. There was no sign of the man on the following evening, but the man-cub came out from the shadows towards us.

We showed him our teeth and he stopped. Then he placed a bag on the ground and backed away into the mist. Father darted forwards and brought the bag back to us. It was full of food. After that, the man-cub came each evening and left food for us. We didn't go close to him because we had seen he was wild.

Then, one evening, the man came back. He waved and we went out to meet him. He had brought all our favourites.

I saw the man-cub in the shadows and trotted towards him but he placed a bag on the ground, then backed away.

Now I am bigger, I hunt on my own.
The man still meets Father, and I meet
the man-cub. He doesn't hunt with the
wild pack any more. He is my friend.

We eat under the stars
and watch the whirlwinds go by.

Other books by Michael Foreman

Cat and Canary
Can't Catch Me!
Cat on the Hill
Dinosaur Time
Norman's Ark
One World
Peter's Place
Surprise! Surprise!
War and Peas
Wonder Goal